P9-BJB-453

FOREST

An I Can Read Book®

FOREST

story by **Laura Godwin**

pictures by **Stacey Schuett**

HarperCollins*Publishers*

HarperCollins®, 🐎®, and I Can Read Book®
are trademarks of HarperCollins Publishers Inc.

Forest
Copyright © 1998 by Laura Godwin
Illustrations copyright © 1998 by Stacey Schuett
Printed in the U.S.A. All rights reserved.

Library of Congress Cataloging-in-Publication Data
Godwin, Laura.
Forest / story by Laura Godwin ; pictures by Stacey Schuett.
    p.   cm. — (An I can read book)
Summary: A young girl hears a noise in the forest near her family's farm in Canada, and
when she and her mother go to investigate, they find a small fawn that seems to be all alone.
ISBN 0-06-026664-3. — ISBN 0-06-026667-8 (lib. bdg.)
[1. Deer—Fiction.   2. Wildlife rescue—Fiction.]   I. Schuett, Stacey, ill.   II. Title.
III. Series.
PZ7.G5438Fo   1998   97-34355
[E]—dc21   CIP
                                                                                    AC

1   2   3   4   5   6   7   8   9   10
❖
First Edition

Visit us on the World Wide Web!
http://www.harperchildrens.com

For Jenna
—L.G.

For Annette
—S.S.

CONTENTS

Chapter One

A NOISE IN THE FOREST

My name is Jeannie.

I live on a farm in Canada.

Every day I help with the chores.

One day I was planting potatoes

in the garden.

There were so many rows!

I thought I would never finish.

I stopped for a rest

and lay down in the grass.

That's when I heard a cry.

"Maa, maa."

"Do you hear that?" I said to Dad.

He was putting new spark plugs

in his tractor.

"Yes," he said.

"It sounds like a baby goat," I said.

"Maybe it is," he said.

"A kid calling for its mother.

It will find her soon enough."

He smiled at me

and rode off on his tractor.

I went back to the garden.

"Maa, maa."

I heard the noise again,

so I put down my hoe

and walked back to the house.

"Mom," I said.

"Come outside and listen."

We heard, "Maa, maa."

"It's coming from the forest,"

she said.

"Let's go see what it is."

Chapter Two

WHAT WE FIND

We climbed over the fence

and walked across the pasture.

We went into the woods.

It was cool and dark.

We saw a chipmunk, two squirrels,

and a huge tree

with lots of pinecones.

Mom walked around it.

I walked under the branches.

"Yuck!" I said. "Spiderwebs."
I brushed them off my face,
but my nose still tickled.
Then I heard something
in front of us.

"What's that?" I asked.

"It's only a bluejay," said Mom,

and she put her arm around me.

Suddenly I saw something else.

19

"Mom, look! A baby deer," I said.

"A fawn."

The fawn was lying in the leaves.

It was brown with white spots

on its back.

"It looks soft," I said.

"Yes," said Mom, "but don't touch it."

"Why not?" I asked.

"If you touch it," Mom said,

"the mother will not come back."

"But it's all alone," I said.

"Maybe," Mom said. "Maybe not.

The doe could be getting food."

Something did not seem right.

I knew Mom felt it too.

We walked back to the house.

All day we heard the fawn cry.

"Maa, maa."

I played inside for a while,

but I could not stop thinking

about the fawn.

After supper I said, "Please, Mom,

can we go see it again?"

"Well . . ." Mom said.

I thought she would say no,

but she said yes.

"I'll come with you," Dad said.

Chapter Three

NOT OURS TO KEEP

We went back to the same spot

in the forest.

"Look," I said.

"It hasn't moved."

"Maa," the fawn said.

"It's not afraid of us," I said.

"It doesn't know it should be afraid,"
Mom said.

"It's only a day or two old."

"Something must have happened

to its mother," Dad said.

"A doe does not let her baby

cry all day."

27

"Can we take it home?" I asked.

"If we take it home," Mom said,

"we will have to feed it

and take care of it.

We cannot keep it, Jeannie.

A wild animal is not ours to keep."

"But if we leave it here,"

I said, "it will die."

I looked at Mom.

She looked at Dad.

He looked at the fawn.

"You are both right," he said.

28

"Maa, maa," the fawn cried again.

"All right," said Mom. "It's late."

"We can take it home and feed it.

But just for tonight."

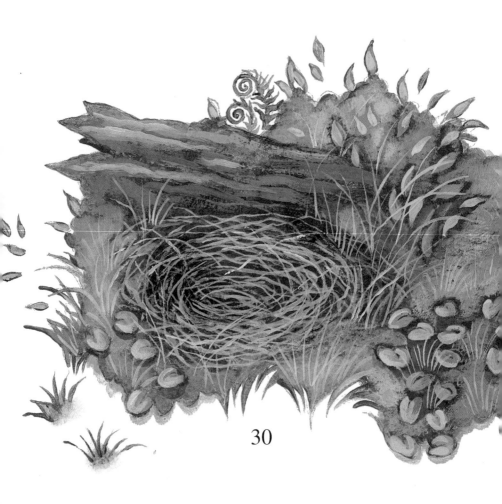

TIME FO

At first th

It lay on

"We need

Dad foun

I got som

"Here's a

"I hope i

I put som

and Dad

We cover

Dad picked it up

and we made our way back

through the forest.

31

"It's a little boy," Dad said.

"He's so tiny," I said.

"Meow," said Gus.

He wanted to see the fawn too.

"Look at him, Gus," I said.

"When he's lying down,

he's not even as big as you."

"If I look after him myself," I said,

"maybe he could stay here

for one more day."

I hoped Mom would say yes,

but she said no.

"Time for bed," she said again.

I walked to the bottom of the stairs.

"Good night," I said.

41

Chapter Five

A GOOD NAME

I lay in bed and waited

until Mom and Dad were asleep.

Then I went downstairs.

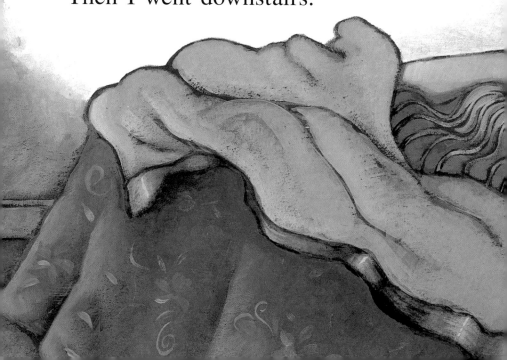

I sat with the fawn

in the dark.

"I have a name for you," I said.

He was quiet.

"It is a good name," I said.

"Your name is Forest,

so you won't forget

where you came from."

I patted his head.

I felt the soft hair

on his ears and said gently,

"I hope you will like

your new home.

I will never forget you, Forest."

I wanted to tell him

that he was safe now.

I wanted to tell him good night,

but my eyes closed.

"Maa," said Forest softly. "Maa."

And we slept.